DATE DUE

GAYLORD		PRINTED IN U.S.A.

COURAGE
OF THE
BLUE BOY

For Kaiser, the best dog ever.

Special thanks to Summer Dawn Laurie & Kara Bang.

 Tricycle Press
an imprint of Ten Speed Press
P.O. Box 7123
Berkeley, California 94707
www.tricyclepress.com

Design by Betsy Stromberg
Typeset in Vag Rounded
The illustrations in this book were done on Arches watercolor paper with brush and India ink and colored on a Macintosh computer with a mouse!

Library of Congress Cataloging-in-Publication Data on file

ISBN-13: 978-1-58246-182-3
ISBN-10: 1-58246-182-1

First Tricycle Press printing, 2006
Printed in China

1 2 3 4 5 6 — 10 09 08 07 06

COURAGE
OF THE
BLUE BOY

ROBERT NEUBECKER

TRICYCLE PRESS
Berkeley • Toronto

There was a blue boy who lived in a blue land.
Everything was blue. Polly the calf was blue.
"There must be more than blue," he sighed.

"Moo," said Polly.

The blue boy dreamed of all the colors of the world.
One day he set off to find them. Polly too.

Blue and Polly rode a yellow bus through a yellow land.

They took a purple taxicab through a purple village.

They flew in an orange airplane over rolling orange hills.

Blue and Polly came to a red town where everyone was red. They lived in red houses and did the same red things, day after day.

Blue wondered, "There must be more than this."

"Moo," said Polly.

They found a land where everything was pink.

Then they crossed a great green ocean.

Finally, they came to a big beautiful city that was unlike any other place they had ever seen.

The houses were red and pink and yellow. The people were green and orange and purple and many other colors. The streets were brown and white, checkered and striped.

There seemed to be every color of shop and every color of newspaper and every color of food to eat.

The blue boy was amazed!
He found a room and moved right in.

Blue and Polly walked up happy amber streets full of colorful people going about their colorful business. They heard maroon sounds. They sniffed olive scents.

They saw the violet museum and went to the emerald opera house. There were scarlet churches, lavender mosques, and beautiful polka-dot temples.

The blue boy loved the colorful city.

Then the blue boy noticed something strange.

He saw no blue.

He looked up every street.
He searched down every alley.
He peeked in every building.

Still no blue. Not here, not there, not anyplace at all.

He grew frightened of the big city.

Blue ran straight to his room. He locked himself in and the city out. He felt safe.

Safe...and bored. "Moo," sighed Polly.

Blue began to pace.
He paced up and down.

And up. And down. Down and up.

Then he had an idea...
a blue idea.

The blue boy pushed his blue idea out under the door.

Then he wrote a blue poem.
He pushed this out too.

He sang a blue song.

He wrote a blue book.

He painted a blue painting,
all for the colorful city.

Finally, Blue got up all of his courage.

He opened the door and peeked outside.

Everywhere he looked there was a little blue. A little blue here on a house, a little blue there on a street corner. Blue pictures, blue books, blue clothes, and blue music!

There were blue leaves on the trees and blue clouds in the sky.
Polly laughed a blue laugh.

Blue began to breathe in all of
the colors of the city, one by one.

They grew inside of him, pink and red and
violet, green and purple and orange, white
and black and yellow.

He wasn't just blue anymore.

He was every color of the world.

And Blue was happy. He knew that wherever he would go in the world, no matter how far, he would always have his big blue heart.

And Polly too.